THE RAVEN BROOKS DISASTER

BY ZAC GORMAN
ILLUSTRATED BY DAVE BARDIN

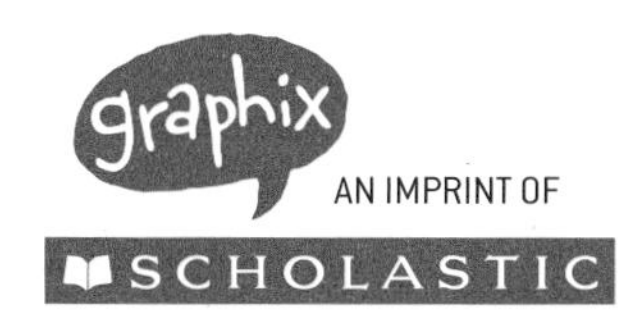

Library of Congress Control Number Available

ISBN 978-1-338-72676-3

10 9 8 7 6 5 4 3 22 23 24 25

Printed in the U.S.A. 40
First edition, August 2021
Edited by Michael Petranek
Art by Dave Bardin
Lettering by Bryan Senka
Book design by Jess Meltzer

"RUFF STUFF" BY C. NOWAK
RUFF! DINNERTIME!
RUFF?
I'M SORRY, WE DON'T DO COAT CHECK!

SIGH.

ROCKY
LUCY
CAT
HEY! HOW'D YOU GET IN HERE?
BABY
JINGLE JINGLE JINGLE JINGLE
OH! FLAN!

OH, FLAN! DON'T BE JEALOUS!
I'M NOT TRYING TO REPLACE YOU! I WOULD NEVER!

PANT
-PANT-
PANT
-PANT-

DON'T YOU TAKE THAT TONE WITH ME, YOUNG MAN.
REGINA! PIZZA'S HERE!

IT'S OKAY! I FORGIVE YOU! WE'RE STILL BEST FRIENDS!

REGINA! PIZZA!
ONE SECOND!

BING-BONG
BING-BONG
BING-BONG
THAT KID, I SWEAR TO GOD . . .
I'M COMING! HOLD ON!
MAYBE RELAX ON THE . . .
. . . DOOR-BELL.
SORRY, I THOUGHT IT WAS BUSTED.
MOST OF THEM ARE.
WAIT, "MOST OF THEM"?
I DIDN'T, UH . . .
SERIOUSLY, IT'S FINE.
DON'T YOU GO TO RAVEN BROOKS HIGH?
OH, UH, NO. NO. NORTH, ACTUALLY.
UGH. EW. A *NORTHMAN.*
WE'RE, UH, NOT THAT BAD. UM, CAN YOU SIGN FOR THIS?
EAGER TO GET BACK OUT INTO THE RAIN, HUH?

NO, I . . .
UH . . .
IT'S, UH, REALLY BAD, ACTUALLY.
RELAX. I'M JOKING.
HUH?
THE RAIN, I MEAN.
THE GUY ON THE RADIO SAID THEY MIGHT HAVE TO EVACUATE THE WHOLE CITY.
NO WAY.
THAT'S WHAT HE . . .
NOPE. I DON'T BUY IT.
REGINA! PIZZA!
IT'S, UH, JUST WHAT HE SAID . . .
DO YOU KNOW MEGHAN LAYTON? SHE GOES TO NORTH.
UH . . . I'M SORRY, I GOTTA . . .
CAN I GET MY PEN BACK?
IT'S MY ONLY ONE.
THE ONLY ONE WITH YOU? OR YOUR ONLY ONE PERIOD?
UH, B-BOTH!

WHO ONLY HAS ONE PEN?
WHAT WERE YOU DOING UP THERE?
NOTHING.

LIKE NOTHING-NOTHING? OR NOTHING-SOMETHING THAT YOU DON'T WANT TO TALK ABOUT?
WHAT'S THE DIFFERENCE?

UH, SEVERAL YEARS OF EXTENSIVE PSYCHO-THERAPY.
HUH?
NOTHING.

YOU SAID SOMETHING.
IT'S JUST THAT YOU'VE BEEN SPENDING A LOT OF TIME IN YOUR ROOM DOING "NOTHING" LATELY.
YOU SOUND LIKE MINDY.
YOU MEAN MOM?
SHE'S YOUR MOM. SHE'S MY MINDY.

IF YOU SAY SO.
WHAT'S SO BAD ABOUT BEING IN MY ROOM, ANYWAY?
I LIKE MY ROOM.

DONSH YOU WANNA GO OUSH WIF YOUR FRIENDSH?

FIRST OF ALL, EW. SWALLOW YOUR FOOD.
SECOND OF ALL, WHAT "FRIENDSH"?

IT'S JUST NOT NORMAL TO . . . YOU KNOW . . .
TO WHAT?

WHAT? YOU WANT MY CRUST?
PANT -PANT- PANT
. . . NEVER MIND.

WE SHOULD AT LEAST PUT SOME MUSIC ON. IT'S SO BORING, YOU'D THINK MOM AND DAD WERE HOME.

SPEAKING OF WHICH, WHEN ARE THEY GETTING BACK?

TOMORROW.
UGH.
TRUST ME. I KNOW.

BUT UNTIL THEN, WE GOTTA MAKE OUR OWN FUN!
COME ON! DANCE WITH ME!
ARF! -ARF!-ARF!- ARF!
GAH! PRIS! STOP!

OH, COME ON! DANCE WITH ME!
SERIOUSLY, PRIS! QUIT IT!
WHY?
ARF! ARF! ARF! ARF!

BECAUSE I HATE IT, OKAY?
PICK ONE!
DANCING OR ME?
ARF! ARF! ARF! ARF!

IT'S OKAY, FLAN.
OH.

I MEAN, IT'S NOT LIKE . . .

IT'S NOT LIKE WE'RE REAL SISTERS, YEAH. WHATEVER.

UH, YEAH. I MEAN . . .

TRUST ME, I DIDN'T ASK FOR THIS, EITHER.
IT'S JUST SINCE . . . EVERYTHING . . .
JUST DROP IT, OKAY? I DON'T LIKE YOU, YOU DON'T LIKE ME.
FINE. WHO CARES? SOON ENOUGH, I'LL BE LEAVING FOR COLLEGE ANYWAY.
BOOST
UH, YEAH. RIGHT.
HM?
BOOST
BZZZ BZZT
WOAH. THE PIZZA GUY WAS RIGHT.
WHAT? WHAT'S GOING ON?
THE MAYOR JUST DECLARED A WEATHER EMERGENCY.
WHAT DOES THAT MEAN?
IT MEANS WE HAVE TO EVACUATE.

HAVE YOU REACHED MOM AND DAD? DID YOU TRY THEIR HOTEL?

I'M LITERALLY CALLING IT RIGHT NOW!
BUT THERE'S SOMETHING WRONG WITH THE PHONES. I DON'T KNOW.

DAMN IT! WHY WON'T YOU WORK?!
MAYBE THE TOWERS ARE DOWN.
WHAT DOES THAT MEAN?

I DON'T KNOW! IT'S JUST WHAT PEOPLE SAY. YOU'RE SUPPOSED TO BE THE ADULT HERE.
THAT DOESN'T MAKE ME A PHONE EXPERT! *UGH!*

YOU WANT ME TO BE THE ADULT? FINE.
GO TO YOUR ROOM AND FINISH PACKING.
WHERE ARE WE GOING?

I DON'T KNOW. IT DOESN'T MATTER.
GO. PACK. NOW.

AND DON'T BRING MORE THAN YOU NEED FOR A DAY OR TWO!
I'LL BRING WHATEVER I WANT!
AND DON'T SLAM YOUR—

SLAM
—DOOR.

SIGH.

YOU COULDN'T HAVE SHOPPED AROUND A LITTLE MORE, MOM?
YOU KNOW, FOUND A NICE GUY WITH LESS BAGGAGE?

I WISH WE'D NEVER COME HERE.
FSHHHHH
PPPPPRRRRRIIIIISSSSSSSSSSH
HUH?
HELLO?

KA-CHHHOW
AAH!
WOAH!
POP
OW!
RUMMMMMMMBLE
OH, COME ON . . .

GOD, SHE HAS NO IDEA WHAT SHE'S DOING! THEY SHOULD'VE LEFT ME IN CHARGE!
ISN'T THAT RIGHT, FLAN?
FLAN? FLAN! WHERE ARE YOU, PAL?
FLAN?
LOST
FLAN!
ARF! ARF! ARF!
DON'T SCARE ME LIKE THAT!
REGINA, ARE YOU READY? I'M— OW!—
I'M TAKING SOME STUFF DOWN TO THE CAR.
BE RIGHT DOWN.

OKAY. HURRY UP, PLEASE.
I SAID, "I'LL BE RIGHT DOWN"!
IT'S OKAY, PAL. WE'RE GONNA BE FINE.
WHY ARE YOU HOLDING EVERYTHING WITH ONE HAND?
BECAUSE I HURT MY WRIST, OKAY? JUST COME ON!
ARE YOU— ARE YOU OKAY?
WHAT DO YOU CARE?
I JUST...
I'M FINE.

SHOULD I RIDE IN THE BACK?
I DON'T CARE. YOU'RE A BIG GIRL, YOU DECIDE.
UGH, I'M GETTING SOAKED!
AAAAH! WET! WET! WET! WET! WET!
ARE YOU SURE YOUR WRIST IS OKAY?
IT'S FINE.
OH, NO!

WHERE ARE YOU GOING?!
I FORGOT SOMETHING! I'LL BE RIGHT BACK!
REGINA! GET BACK HERE! **REGINA!**
THAT KID! I SWEAR!
HUH?
I COULD'VE SWORN . . .

CH-KUNK
AAH!
GOT IT!
OH, MY GOD! YOU SCARED ME!
WAIT. WHY DO YOU . . .
I ALMOST FORGOT FLAN'S FAVORITE BOWL!
FLAN
WHAT? WHAT'S THAT LOOK FOR?
NOTHING. NOTHING. LET'S JUST GO.
IT'S OKAY, PAL.
ARF!

281 • NEI

RAVEN BROOKS
Next 2 Exits
WHERE ARE WE GOING?
AWAY.
NOT IN A HURRY, APPARENTLY.
OH, I'M SORRY. DO YOU WANT TO DRIVE?
I'D DO A BETTER JOB.
WE SHOULD GO TO THE HOTEL.
MOM AND DAD'S HOTEL? WE CAN'T.
WHY?
BECAUSE I DON'T KNOW WHERE IT IS AND MY PHONE IS USELESS.
QUIT DISTRACTING ME.

WE SHOULD'VE JUST STAYED HOME! IT'S JUST SOME STUPID RAIN!
NOW WE'RE DRIVING TO THE MIDDLE OF NOWHERE IN A STORM!
HOW IS THIS ANY SAFER?
ARF! ARF! ARF!
FLAN? YOU ALL RIGHT, PAL? DO YOU NEED TO GO TO THE BATHROOM?
OH, MY GOD. SIT. DOWN.
HE HAS TO GO TO THE BATHROOM!
CAN YOU NOT DO THIS NOW, REGINA?
DO WHAT?
JUST KNOCK IT OFF!
KNOCK WHAT OFF? FLAN NEEDS TO GO TO THE BATHROOM!
DAMN IT, REGINA! FLAN IS—

WHAT THE—!
AAAAAAAAAAAAAAAAAAAAAAAHH!
NO-NO-NO-NO-NO!
STOP IT! STOP IT!
WE'RE GONNA—

PANT
-PANT-
PANT
-PANT-
YIP!
YIP!
YIP!
SHHH! KUIIT!
KPPP KUIIT, PAL! YRR'R SPOSED TU B A SIRPIS!
YIP! YIP!
YIP! YIP!
YIP!

HUKNEE? RRGNNA? M HMM!
SHHH!
YIP! YIP!

DD? WHUDS TADT?
YIP! YIP! YIP!

SS TADT A . . . DGG?

TT'S A DGG! TT'S A DGG!

THNNK UUU! THNNK UUU! TT'S A DGG!
YIP! YIP! YIP!

S TADT A DGG? WHE TKKKED ABTT TSSS!
OO, M SURREE FRR MKNNG MI DTTRR HAPPY.
GEZSS, DNN.

YIP! YIP! YIP! YIP!
OOO'S A GDD BUOY?
OOO'S A GDD BUOY?

HAHAHA!

M NVVRR GOON TO LTT UUU GO, PAL!

YIP! YIP!

KREEEE
281 • NEI
KOFF KOFF
R-REGINA?
REGINA!
281 • NEI
OVER HERE!
ARE YOU OKAY?
I'M FINE. FLAN . . . HE'S . . . HE'S JUST SCARED.
281 • NEI

I'M JUST GLAD YOU'RE ALL RIGHT.
UH . . . BOTH OF YOU.
Y-YEAH. THANKS.
GOD, WHAT HAPPENED?
THERE WAS . . . SOMETHING IN THE ROAD. DIDN'T YOU SEE IT?
NO. WHAT WAS IT?
IT LOOKED LIKE— UH . . . NEVER MIND. IT WAS PROBABLY NOTHING.
SO, NOW WHAT?
WELL, I DON'T THINK I COULD PUSH THE CAR OUT OF THIS DITCH EVEN IF I HAD TWO GOOD WRISTS.
SO, THAT MEANS . . .
. . . WE'RE STUCK?
WE'RE STUCK.

UGGGHHHHHHH!
THAT'S NOT HELPING.
I TOLD YOU WE NEVER SHOULD'VE LEFT HOME!
I'LL THINK OF SOMETHING.
LIKE WHAT?
I. DON'T. KNOW. *SOMETHING.*
WELL, THANKS FOR NOT BEING VAGUE.
CAR! CAR!
HEY! OVER HERE! OVER HERE!

GOLDEN APPLE AMUSEMENT PARK
HEY! WE'RE OVER HERE!
OH, MY OD! WHAT A RELIEF!
E SKIDDED F THE ROAD AND WE'RE STUCK!
I WASN'T SURE ANYBODY WAS GOING TO COME BY!
SOME NIGHT TO GET STUCK.
Y-YEAH.
DO YOU HAVE A PHONE THAT WORKS?
YOURS DOESN'T?

I MEAN, SURE IT DOES. BUT WE'RE CHARGING IT.
MY SISTER IS. SHE'S, UH, IN THE CAR.
WITH OUR DOG. OUR BIG, STRONG GUARD DOG.
HM. WELL, IF YOU NEED A RIDE TO THE NEAREST GAS STATION, I'LL TAKE YOU.
I WON'T TWIST YOUR ARM. IT'S YOUR CHOICE.
FINE. DEAL.
BUT I WANT YOU TO KNOW THAT MY DAD'S A COP AND MY MOM'S A FORMER MARINE.
UNDERSTOOD.
COME ON. HE'S GIVING US A RIDE.
YOU MEAN THE TOTAL STRANGER IN THE KIDNAPPER VAN?
IT'S A MOVING TRUCK.
OH. MUCH BETTER.

UH, WHAT ABOUT YOUR DOG?
DON'T WORRY ABOUT IT. LET'S GO.
SURE THING.

SO, WHAT ARE YOU HAULING?
EXCUSE ME?
I SAID, "WHAT ARE YOU HAULING"?
YOU MUST BE IN A HURRY TO GET THERE, DRIVING ON A NIGHT LIKE TONIGHT.
UHH . . .
REGINA!

SORRY. SHE'S NOSY.
NO. IT'S FINE. TRUST ME. I KNOW ALL ABOUT NOSY KIDS.
OH, YEAH. THAT'S NOT OMINOUS OR ANYTHING.

I WAS MOVING BEFORE THE STORM CAME.
I WAS ALREADY PACKED UP WHEN THE CALL TO EVACUATE WENT OUT.

I GUESS YOU'RE JUST LUCKY— HEY! FLAN! QUIT IT!
SNUFF -SNUFF- -SNUFF- SNUFF!
WHO'S FLAN?
OH, MY GOD.
WHAT'S IN THERE, PAL? WHAT DO YOU SMELL?
NO!
KLATCH
ARF!
IT'S—UH—THAT STUFF IS P-PERSONAL. PLEASE. LEAVE IT ALONE.
H-HEY! LOOK! WHAT'S THAT?

JUST STAY HERE. I'LL GO SEE WHAT'S GOING ON.
UH, SHOULDN'T WE GO? MY CAR . . .
DON'T BE RIDICULOUS! NO REASON FOR ALL OF US TO GET SOAKED.
I'LL TELL HIM ALL ABOUT YOUR CAR AND ASK WHAT WE SHOULD DO.
BUT . . .
STAY HERE.

HE'S UP TO SOME-THING.
WHO?
HEY! WHAT ARE YOU DOING?
SHHH!
GAH!
KRAWWK
WHAT THE HECK WAS THAT?
WHO KEEPS A BIRD IN THEIR GLOVE BOX?!

HOW NAÏVE ARE YOU, REGINA? HE'S DEFINITELY UP TO SOMETHING!
AND HE'S DEFINITELY COMING THIS WAY.
CRAP! JUST ACT NORMAL, OKAY?
HE SAID— UH, IS SOMETHING WRONG?
N-NOTHING!
RIGHT. ANYWAY, ROAD'S CLOSED. HE SAID THERE'S A GAS STATION JUST A LITTLE WAYS FROM HERE.
SAID I MIGHT AS WELL GIVE YOU A RIDE MYSELF, SINCE IT'D BE A WHILE BEFORE AN OFFICER COULD GET OUT HERE TO PICK YOU GIRLS UP.
UH, ARE YOU SURE?
EXCUSE ME?
I MEAN, ARE YOU SURE YOU DON'T MIND? WE COULD WAIT HERE. IT'S NO PROBLEM.
NO.

IT'S NO PROBLEM. NONE AT ALL.
YOU, UH, YOU NEVER TOLD US YOUR NAME.
NO? HUH. COULD'VE SWORN I DID.
YOU CAN CALL ME MR. PETERSON.
POLICE

Cash
Credit/Debit
375 385
385 395
395 405
I'M JUST GOING TO FILL UP.
UH-HUH. SURE. YEP.
WHAT ABOUT FLAN?
IS FLAN GOING TO BE OKAY BY HIMSELF?
YEP. YEAH. COME ON.
EXCUSE ME. HI. HELLO.

DO YOU HAVE A PHONE WE COULD USE?
A WHAT?
I FEEL WEIRD LEAVING FLAN OUT THERE.
A PHONE. SHORT FOR *TELEPHONE*. YOU KNOW, THE THING YOU CALL PEOPLE ON?
SORRY. NO PHONE.
PRIS. HEY, PRIS. I'M WORRIED ABOUT FLAN.
WHO?
MY DOG.
WE'VE BEEN KIDNAPPED. CAN WE PLEASE USE YOUR PHONE?
WE WEREN'T KIDNAPPED. HE WAS JUST GIVING US A RIDE.
SO, WERE YOU OR WEREN'T YOU KIDNAPPED?
REGINA! A WORD?

HEY! WHAT ARE YOU DOING?
ME? WHAT ARE *YOU* DOING?

IN CASE YOU FORGOT, I'M IN CHARGE!
YOU LIED TO HER! MR. PETERSON DIDN'T KIDNAP US!
OH, MY GOD!

I LIED BECAUSE WE'RE IN TROUBLE AND YOU'RE TOO DUMB TO REALIZE IT!
YOU'RE SO PROTECTED! WE ALL WALK ON EGGSHELLS AROUND YOU AND TREAT YOU LIKE YOU'RE A BABY, AND I'M SICK OF IT!

DON'T CALL ME A BABY! THIS IS YOUR FAULT! WE SHOULD'VE STAYED HOME WHERE WE WERE SAFE!

IF YOU DON'T WANT ME TO CALL YOU A BABY, THEN STOP ACTING LIKE A BABY!
HEY! WHERE ARE YOU GOING?
TO GET FLAN.
OH. MY. GOD.

"OH, MY GOD," WHAT? WHAT? JUST SAY IT. WHAT?

REGINA. COME ON.
SAY IT. JUST SAY IT.
QUIT IT.

SAY IT. *SAY IT!*

REGINA . . . FLAN'S DEAD.

REGINA. I'M SORRY. IT'S TRUE.

I HATE YOU. I HATE YOU. I HATE YOU.

REGINA, WAIT!

HOLD ON, THERE, YOUNG LADY.
GET OUT OF MY WAY! MY SISTER'S OUT THERE!

YOU SAID THAT YOU TWO WERE BEING KIDNAPPED.
DO YOU KNOW HOW SERIOUS THAT IS? WE HAVE TO CALL THE POLICE.
HAVE TO.

HOW?! ALL THE PHONES ARE DEAD!

HELLO?
HELLO? ANYBODY HERE?
ARF!
FLAN?
FLAN? ARE YOU IN THERE?
WHAT IS ALL THIS STUFF?
ARF! ARF!
FLAN! I'M COMING, PAL! HOLD ON!

YOU WANNA TELL US WHAT'S GOING ON?
LEAVE ME ALONE!

REGINA!

OH, NO.

OOF!
WHAM

WAIT! WAIT! REGINA!
REGINA!
NO. NO. NO. NO. NO. NO. NO.
UH, ARE YOU OKAY?
NO. NO. NO. NO. NO. NO. NO. NO.
COME ON. LET'S GET INSIDE.
NO. NO. NO. REGINA. NO.

HAPP
BIRTHD

UUU KNOO Y SHSS HDDNG.
HRR UEE GOO. BLMM ME. AGNN.

WLLL, THUH PRRTEES ROOND.
OOO CRRSS? REGINA DUZNT.
ARF!

MM NUT GVVNG UUU PZZZUH.
GTT LAWST. GO FIND REGINA.

ARF!

GO AWAY.
FNN. WHUDVR. STAY.
ARF!

FLAN?
ARF!

FLAN? ARE YOU THERE?
ARF!

IT'S A TOY.
ARF! ARF! ARF!

HEY! WAIT! I'M IN HERE!
SLAM!

WAIT! WAIT! WA—
VARUMRUMRUMRUMRUMRUM

—AIT! OOF!
WE'RE MOVING!
DAMN IT! STOP!
HUH?
WHAT THE HECK?
WEIRD.

WOAH. IT'S A NEST.

YOUR SISTER'S IN THE TRUCK?
THAT'S WHAT I'VE BEEN TRYING TO TELL YOU!

IF YOU HADN'T GOTTEN IN MY WAY, I MIGHT'VE STOPPED HER BEFORE IT WAS TOO LATE!
JUST CALM DOWN.

YOU CALM— *OW! OW! OW!*

I'M A NURSE. LET ME SEE.

CAN YOU MOVE IT? OKAY. THAT'S GOOD.
DO YOU HAVE ANY MEDICAL STUFF HERE?

THINK WE MIGHT HAVE SOME WRIST BRACES OVER THERE.
OH, GOOD.

GIMME THAT LOOK ALL YOU WANT, SWEETIE.
IT'S NOT GONNA FIX ANYTHING.

HERE. GIVE ME YOUR ARM.

HOW'S THAT FEEL? BETTER?
Y-YEAH. BETTER. THANKS.

THAT'LL BE $12.99.

GET BENT.
EXCUSE ME?

OKAY, LET'S ALL CALM DOWN.
YOU'RE USELESS! BOTH OF YOU! THIS IS ALL YOUR FAULT!
LISTEN, I WAS ONLY TRYING TO GET THE FACTS STRAIGHT.
YOUR SISTER SAID YOU WERE FINE.

PLEASE. WE HAVE TO DO SOMETHING! REGINA . . .
YOU'RE RIGHT. WE REALLY SHOULD CALL THE POLICE.

CAN'T. PHONE'S DEAD, REMEMBER?

SORRY, BUT IT LOOKS LIKE YOU'RE GONNA HAVE TO HOLD TIGHT UNTIL THE STORM PASSES.

DAMN IT!
CRASH

HEY! WHAT THE—
EASY! RELAX! SHE'S JUST A KID!
YOU'RE GONNA PAY FOR ANYTHING THAT'S BROKEN!

IF ANYTHING IS DAMAGED, I'LL PAY FOR IT. OKAY? OKAY?
WHATEVER.

YOU CAN WRECK UP THE PLACE, SWEETIE, BUT IT ISN'T GONNA BRING YOUR SISTER BACK.
GO TO HELL.

OH, HONEY. I'M SURE YOUR SISTER IS FINE.

YOU'RE NOT THE FIRST PERSON WHO'S LOST SOMEONE.
AND I DON'T MEAN "LOST" LIKE GREW APART FROM OR EVEN DIED. I MEAN *LOST.*
TELL ME. YOU EVER HEARD OF THE RAVEN MAN?

WHAT DO YOU KNOW?

DO YOU *REALLY* THINK THIS IS APPROPRIATE?
THE WHAT?

THE RAVEN MAN. AN UNINVITED GUEST THAT COMES AT NIGHT TO TAKE AWAY THE THINGS WE LOVE.
HAVE YOU HEARD THE OLD RHYME?
"1, 2, 3, 4 . . . RAVEN MAN IS AT YOUR DOOR . . ."

I'VE SEEN HIM! THE RAVEN MAN!
EMPLOYEES ONLY
OH, COME ON. IT'S AN *URBAN LEGEND.* NOT EVEN A CLEVER ONE. WE LIVE IN *RAVEN BROOKS,* HENCE *RAVEN MAN.* BRILLIANT. IT'S JUST A STORY.

I'M SORRY I DIDN'T BELIEVE YOU.
WHERE CAN WE FIND HIM?
WHO?
THE RAVEN MAN.

THIS IS RIDICULOUS. YOU'RE COMING WITH ME.
DON'T LISTEN TO THIS NON-SENSE.
WHAT? HUH?

DO YOU HAVE ANY IDEA WHERE THEY WERE GOING?
NO, BUT . . .
WELL THEN, SINCE NOBODY SEEMS TO HAVE A WORKING PHONE, I'LL DRIVE YOU TO THE POLICE STATION MYSELF.
O-OKAY.

HEY! I THOUGHT YOU WERE GONNA PAY FOR THIS?
HERE . . .

KEEP THE CHANGE.

JUST A LITTLE FARTHER . . .
FINALLY!

IT'S ME—
AND FLAN.
YOU USED TO BE SO HAPPY.
BUT YOU DIDN'T WANT HIM ANYMORE. SO, I TOOK HIM AWAY.
LIAR! I WOULD NEVER! I LOVE HIM!
NO. YOU LOVED HIM. PAST TENSE.
NOW HE'S GONE AND YOU'VE FORGOTTEN HIM. MOVED ON.
IT'S FOR THE BEST, HONESTLY. IT WAS GETTING EMBARRASSING.

SHUT UP!
YOU'RE TOO OLD FOR IMAGINARY FRIENDS . . .
AND A DEAD PET, AT THAT . . .
HOW *MORBID*, HOW *CHILDISH.*
YOU'RE SUCH A BABY, REGINA.
JUST SHUT UP! YOU'RE— YOU'RE . . .
I'M NOT A BABY! AND I DIDN'T FORGET ABOUT FLAN! I LOVE HIM!
HA HA! OKAY, THEN! LET'S SEE HIM!
WHAT'S WRONG? SOMETHING NOT WORKING?
SHUT UP!

CAN'T DO IT, CAN YOU?
YOU SHOULD BE HAPPY!
YOU DON'T NEED AN IMAGINARY DOG ANYMORE.
IT WAS SO SAD. SO PATHETIC.
GO AWAY.
TELL YOU WHAT. I'LL HELP YOU OUT . . .
THERE YOU GO! GOOD AS NEW!
ARF! ARF!
FLAN!
WHAT?
HAHAHAHA!
THAT'S NOT FLAN. AND YOU'RE NOT PRIS.
WAKE UP.
NO? THEN WHO AM I?

HM.

YOU KNOW, IN ALL THE CONFUSION, I'M NOT SURE I EVEN HAD A CHANCE TO INTRODUCE MYSELF.
I'M JULIE.

I'M PRIS.

WHERE ARE YOUR PARENTS? DO THEY KNOW YOU'RE OUT HERE?
THEY'RE GONE FOR THE NIGHT.
IT'S THEIR FIRST ANNIVERSARY AND MOM WANTED TO MAKE IT "SPECIAL." PFFT.
SO, THEY'RE . . .
REMARRIED. YEAH.
REGINA'S MY STEPSISTER. I WAS TRYING TO MAKE IT WORK BUT SHE . . .
I DON'T KNOW. SHE'S NOT EASY. WE HAVE NOTHING IN COMMON.
AND LAST YEAR, JUST AFTER THE WEDDING, HER DOG DIED.
OH, NO.
YOU HAVE NO DEA. SHE LOVED THAT DOG.
I'M PRETTY SURE HE GOT HER THROUGH HER PARENTS' DIVORCE, WHICH FROM WHAT I'VE HEARD WAS, UH, MESSY.
SINCE THEN, SHE'S JUST BEEN SO . . . OUT OF IT.
GOD. POOR KID.

I JUST DON'T KNOW WHAT TO DO.
IS IT UP TO YOU?
HUH?
I MEAN, ISN'T THERE SOMEONE ELSE REGINA CAN TALK TO?
NOT REALLY. DAD'S BUSY.
ALL HER FRIENDS SORT OF ABANDONED HER ONCE SHE DECIDED TO GO ON PRETENDING THAT FLAN —THAT WAS HER DOG— WAS STILL ALIVE.
I THINK IT CREEPED THEM OUT.
THAT IS PRETTY . . . DARK.
YOU KNOW, YOU'D THINK SO? BUT IT WAS ACTUALLY KINDA CUTE.
AND PRETENDING HE WAS STILL AROUND MADE HER HAPPY, SO WHAT'S THE HARM IN THAT?
I GUESS MAYBE YOU'D HAVE TO KNOW REGINA.

I JUST— I JUST HOPE SHE'S ALL RIGHT.
HEY! HEY! I'M SURE SHE'S FINE!
LIKE YOU SAID, THE GUY WAS CREEPY BUT YOU DON'T KNOW THAT HE WAS DANGEROUS.
MAYBE HE DIDN'T SEE YOUR SISTER GET IN THE BACK. MAYBE THIS IS ALL A BIG MISUNDER-STANDING.
YEAH, SURE. OR MAYBE THE RAVEN MAN GOT HER.
PFFT!
THAT WOMAN! I SWEAR, I SHOULD'VE PUNCHED HER IN THE MOUTH, SAYING THAT GARBAGE.
YOU MIGHT AS WELL SAY BIGFOOT TOOK YOUR SISTER.
HA, YEAH. MAYBE.
AW, CRUD!

NOW WHAT?
I GUESS WE'VE GOTTA FIND ANOTHER WAY TO THE STATION.
DON'T WORRY. WE'LL GET THERE.

I SAID, "WAKE UP."
I DON'T LIKE STOWAWAYS. ESPECIALLY WHEN THEY'RE NOSY LITTLE KIDS.
WHAT'S GOING ON?
I DON'T HAVE TIME FOR THIS. I'LL FIGURE OUT WHAT TO DO WITH YOU LATER.
WHERE ARE WE?
WAIT! DON'T LEAVE ME IN HERE!
THAT'S WHAT YOU THINK.
CRAP!

HUH? WHAT'S THAT?
WEIRD.
COOL. IT'S A LIGHT.
IT'S A LOT LESS SCARY IN THE LIGHT.

THE NEST IS GONE, TOO, BUT THERE'S SOMETHING . . .
BINGO!
KAW!
KAW!
KAW!
KAW!
KAW!
KAW!
KAW!
WHAT IS THIS PLACE?

IT'S SOME SORT OF OLD WEATHER STATION.

WHAT THE . . .?

BEAUTIFUL, ISN'T IT?
KAW!
KAW!

NOW HE'S TALKING TO THE BIRD? THAT CAN'T BE GOOD.

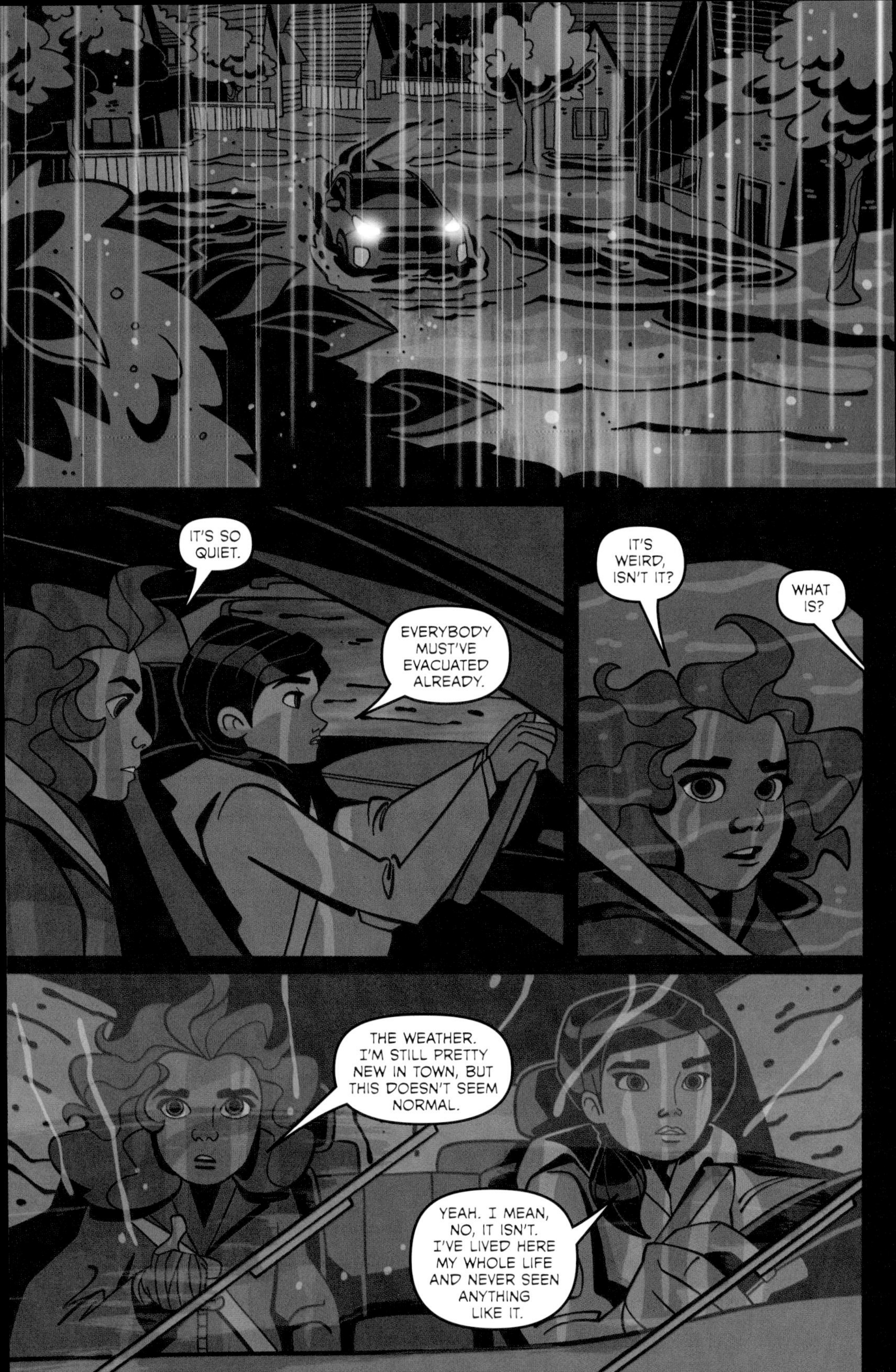
IT'S SO QUIET.
EVERYBODY MUST'VE EVACUATED ALREADY.
IT'S WEIRD, ISN'T IT?
WHAT IS?
THE WEATHER. I'M STILL PRETTY NEW IN TOWN, BUT THIS DOESN'T SEEM NORMAL.
YEAH. I MEAN, NO, IT ISN'T. I'VE LIVED HERE MY WHOLE LIFE AND NEVER SEEN ANYTHING LIKE IT.

THESE THINGS HAPPEN, I GUESS. GLOBAL WARMING. WHO KNOWS?
IS THAT WHAT YOU THINK? GLOBAL WARMING?
MAYBE. I DON'T KNOW.
I MEAN, IT'S WEATHER, RIGHT? IT'S UNPREDICTABLE.
HM. I GUESS.
UH-OH. ROAD'S OUT HERE, TOO.
CAN WE GO THROUGH IT?
I DON'T KNOW. WE HAVE NO IDEA HOW DEEP THAT THING IS . . .

WE CAN'T TURN AROUND AGAIN! WHO KNOWS WHAT'S HAPPENING TO REGINA RIGHT NOW! PLEASE!
PRIS . . .
WE'RE NOT GOING TO GET THERE ANY FASTER IF WE GET STUCK.
PLEASE . . . WE HAVE TO TRY . . .
FINE.
WE'RE GOING THROUGH.
WE'VE GOT THIS! TRUST ME.
I HOPE YOU'RE RIGHT.

READY?
READY.

VROOOOOOOOOO
KA-SPLASH!

WE'RE DOING IT!
WE'RE GONNA MAKE IT!
VRRRRRRRRRRRRRRRR

WHAT IS THAT? WHAT'S THAT NOISE?
VRRRRRRR-RRR-R
SPLUT
-SPLUT-
SPLUT

SPLLT-SPLLT-SPL-SP---KLUNK
NO! THE ENGINE STALLED!
AH! WHAT DO WE DO? WHAT DO WE DO?
ROLL DOWN THE WINDOW AND CLIMB OUT!
JULIE! HELP!
I'M COMING!
AUGH! IT'S SO COLD!
COME ON. ALMOST THERE.
I'M SORRY. I'M SO SORRY.

WE DIDN'T MAKE IT.
NO.
WE DIDN'T MAKE IT.

CLOSE THE DOOR. IT'S COLD.
SO, WHAT'S IT DO?
ISN'T IT OBVIOUS?
NOT EVEN A LITTLE.
ARE YOU FAMILIAR WITH THE CONCEPT OF CLOUD SEEDING? ICE NUCLEATION? THE BERGERON PROCESS?
I'M ELEVEN.
FINE. IT WAS WRONGHEADED ANYWAY.
AT LEAST THE WAY THEY WERE GOING ABOUT IT WAS. BUT I FIGURED IT OUT.
DOPPLER COOLING ON A MASSIVE SCALE.
AGAIN. ELEVEN.

FINE. I'LL KEEP IT SIMPLE THEN . . . WEATHER CONTROL.
YOU CAUSED THE STORM? WHY?
BECAUSE SOMETIMES THE ONLY WAY THROUGH IS FORWARD.
KAW! KAW! KAW!
WHAT IS IT?
KRRRAW!
INTERESTING. INTERESTING.
NOW, WHERE WAS I? RIGHT. RIGHT.
WE ALL HAVE OUR LOT IN LIFE. I USED TO WANT TO CHANGE THE PAST, BUT YOU CAN'T, CAN YOU?
ALL YOU CAN DO IS BUILD A NEW FUTURE.
BY WHAT, FLOODING THE TOWN?
CAN'T MAKE AN OMELET WITHOUT BREAKING A FEW EGGS, RIGHT?
NO OFFENSE INTENDED.
KAW!
THE CIRCUIT BREAKER?

THERE'S SOMETHING WRONG WITH THE CIRCUIT BREAKER . . .
BUT WHY RAVEN BROOKS?
WHY NOT? I NEEDED TO TEST MY MACHINE AND HERE I AM. LOOKS LIKE IT WORKS A BIT TOO WELL, HONESTLY.
BUT . . .
BUT, BUT, BUT! YOU KEEP LOOKING FOR A REASON! LISTEN TO ME, BAD THINGS HAPPEN WITHOUT REASON.
ENTROPY! EVERYTHING MOVES TOWARD CHAOS AND DISORDER! THINGS ARE STOLEN FROM US.
PEOPLE ARE TAKEN. THERE. IS. NO. REASON.
NOW, IF YOU'LL EXCUSE ME, I NEED TO CHECK SOMETHING IN THE BASEMENT.
IF I WERE YOU, I'D BE GONE BY THE TIME I GET BACK.
CLOMP-CLOMP-CLOMP-CLOMP-CLOMP
OH, NO . . .
ZWOOP
EEEEEEEEEEEEEEE!
WHOOOOOOOOOOOOOOSH!

HELLO? IS ANYBODY HOME?
UGH. I CAN'T REMEMBER THE LAST TIME I WAS DRY.
OH, IT'S OPEN!
HELLO? ANYBODY HOME? OUR CAR IS STUCK! IF YOU'RE HERE, WE'RE NOT MURDERERS!
THAT'S EXACTLY WHAT A MURDERER WOULD SAY.
POWER'S OUT. NOT A SURPRISE.
IT'S SO WEIRD . . .

WHAT IS?
BEING IN SOMEONE ELSE'S HOUSE WHEN THEY'RE AWAY LIKE THIS.
NOT FOR ME. I USED TO DO IT ALL THE TIME. JUST A LITTLE B 'N' E, NO BIG DEAL.
WHAT?
JOKING.
I'M GONNA GO FIND THE BATHROOM. HOPEFULLY THE TOILET STILL WORKS.
ARF!

ARF! ARF! ARF! ARF!
HELLO?
ARF! ARF!
ARF! ARF! ARF!

FLAN?

ARF!
-ARF!-ARF!-
ARF!

ARF! ARF! ARF!
FLAN! WAIT!
WAIT! FLAN! STAY!
STAY! STAY, YOU STUPID DOG!
STOP, FLAN! STOP!
ARF! ARF! ARF!
DAMN IT!

STUPID DOG.

FLAN? FLAN? COMM UN, PAL!

THRRR UU RR, PAL! COMM UN!

HAY, SURRY YURR NTT FLLING WLLL, PAL.

YHEA, DNN'T BOTTR HULPNNG RR NYTTING.

YU WNNT MR. BUNNY?

SRRRY, FLAN.

MM SOW SRRRY, PAL.

I NNOE TT'S BAYD. I NNOE.
MM SOW SRRRY YUU'RR SIKK.

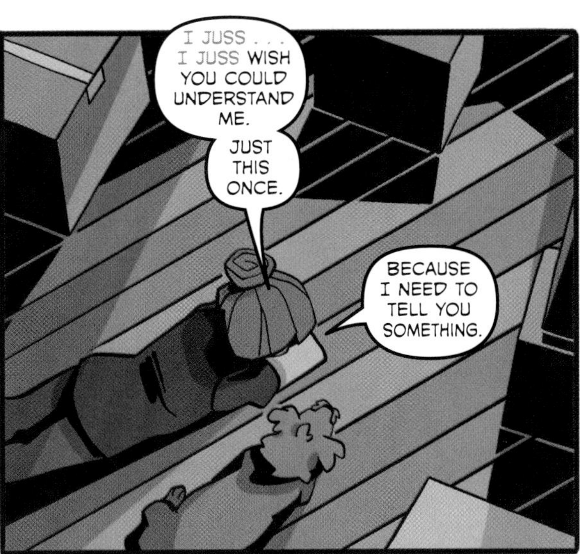
I JUSS . . . I JUSS WISH YOU COULD UNDERSTAND ME.
JUST THIS ONCE.
BECAUSE I NEED TO TELL YOU SOMETHING.

I'M SORRY.
I'M SORRY FOR EVERY TIME WE DIDN'T PLAY TOGETHER OR THAT I DIDN'T GIVE YOU MY SCRAPS AT DINNER.
I'M SO SORRY.

DAD SAYS YOU'RE SICK AND SUFFERING BUT YOU'RE MY BEST FRIEND AND I CAN'T LOSE YOU.
I CAN'T. I LOVE YOU SO MUCH.

PLEASE. PLEASE. I LOVE YOU SO MUCH.
YOU NEED TO KNOW THAT. YOU NEED TO KNOW.

TAP TAP TAP TAP TAP TAP TAP

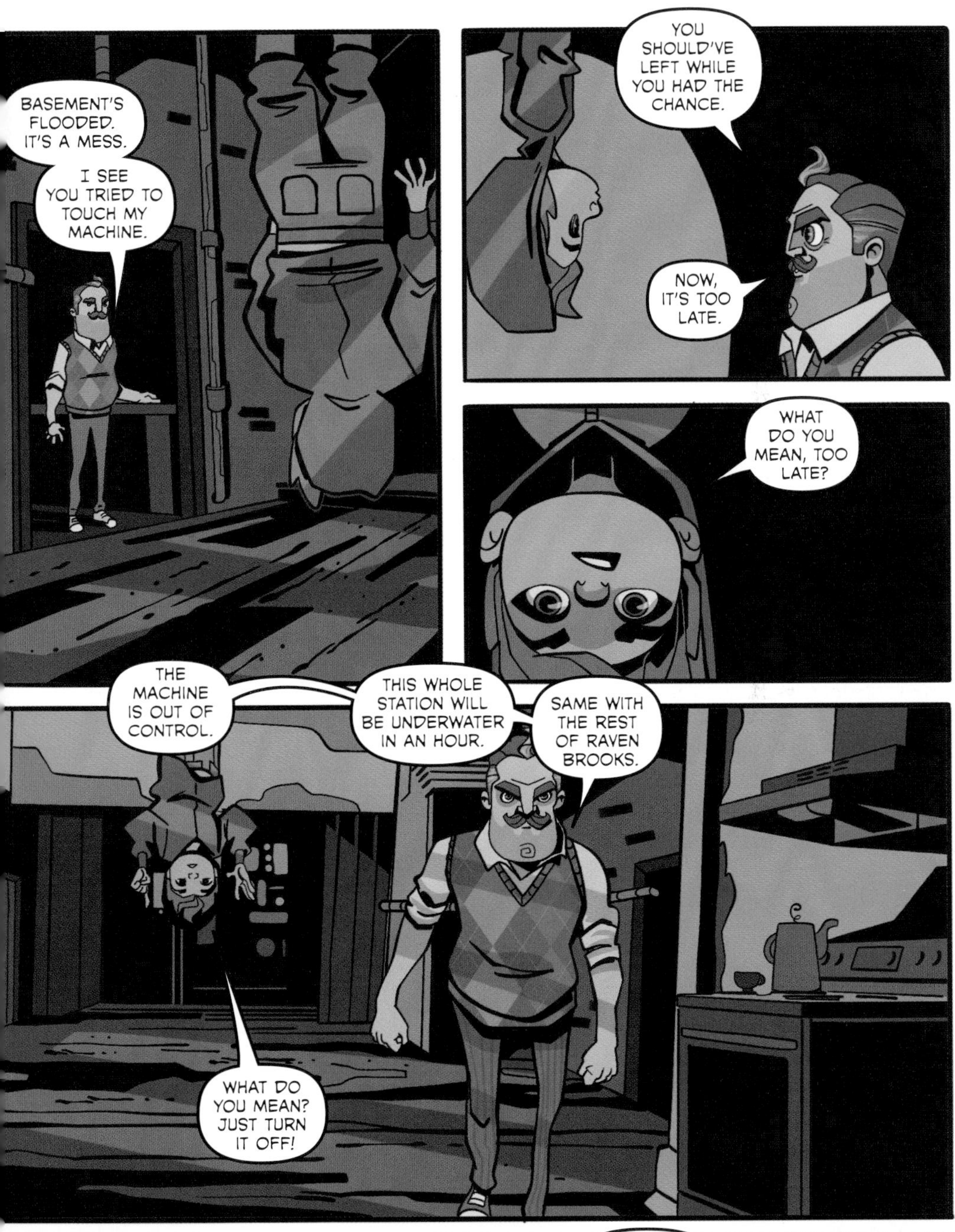
BASEMENT'S FLOODED. IT'S A MESS.
I SEE YOU TRIED TO TOUCH MY MACHINE.
YOU SHOULD'VE LEFT WHILE YOU HAD THE CHANCE.
NOW, IT'S TOO LATE.
WHAT DO YOU MEAN, TOO LATE?
THE MACHINE IS OUT OF CONTROL.
THIS WHOLE STATION WILL BE UNDERWATER IN AN HOUR.
SAME WITH THE REST OF RAVEN BROOKS.
WHAT DO YOU MEAN? JUST TURN IT OFF!

EVEN IF I COULD, I'M NOT SURE THAT I WOULD.
BESIDES, THE ENTIRE TOWN IS EVACUATED. NO ONE WILL DIE NEEDLESSLY.

WHAT ABOUT US? WHAT ABOUT MY SISTER? SHE'S PROBABLY OUT THERE LOOKING FOR ME, RIGHT NOW!
OR SHE'S SAFELY EVACUATED. EITHER WAY, IT DOESN'T MATTER. LIKE I SAID, I CAN'T TURN IT OFF.
CUT THE POWER!
NO.

WHY?!
BECAUSE IT WOULD RUIN MY MACHINE AND, MORE IMPORTANTLY, BECAUSE I DON'T WANT TO.

HAVE YOU CONSIDERED THAT MAYBE YOUR TOWN DESERVES TO FLOOD?
MAYBE THEN THE INGRATES WHO LIVE HERE WILL FINALLY UNDERSTAND WHAT IT MEANS TO LOSE SOMETHING!
NOBODY APPRECIATES ANYTHING UNTIL IT'S GONE!

YOU. YOU'RE THE RAVEN MAN.

WHAT, HAT DO YOU . . .
THE LOCAL LEGEND.
YOU TAKE WHAT OTHER PEOPLE DON'T APPRECIATE.

EVERYBODY'S ALWAYS SO FOCUSED ON WHAT THE RAVEN MAN TAKES FROM THEM, THEY NEVER STOP TO THINK ABOUT WHY HE TAKES IT.
HE TAKES THINGS AWAY BECAUSE HE'S LONELY.

THAT'S WHY, ISN'T IT? ISN'T THAT WHY YOU TAKE THINGS? BECAUSE YOU'RE LONELY?
BECAUSE YOU WANT OTHER PEOPLE TO FEEL THE PAIN THAT YOU'VE FELT?
YOU DON'T HAVE TO BE LIKE THIS! THERE'S STILL TIME TO MAKE THINGS RIGHT!

PLEASE. TURN OFF THE MACHINE.
I-I CAN'T.
PLEASE.

I . . .
PLEASE.

FLAN! FLAN!
ARF! ARF! ARF!
UGH! YUCK!
ARF! ARF! ARF!
HOLD ON, PAL! I'M COMING!
ARF! ARF!

MR. PETERSON! HOW'S IT GOING DOWN THERE?
NOT GOOD! THE BREAKER'S TOTALLY UNDER-WATER!
I'M GOING TO HAVE TO DIVE TO CUT THE POWER!
NOT SURE HOW TO DO THAT WITHOUT ELECTROCUTING MYSELF!
YOU'RE DOING THE RIGHT THING!
HMPF.

BLUB-BLUB

FLAN. FLAN. COME ON. THIS IS SO FAR.
I GIVE UP. I'M GONNA DIE HERE.
I'M JUST GONNA LIE DOWN IN A DITCH AND DIE. IS THAT COOL?
HUH?

UH, MR. PETERSON? HELLO?
IT'S BEEN A WHILE SINCE I HEARD ANYTHING DOWN THERE! YOU OKAY?
THAT'S NOT GOOD.
THAT'S REALLY NOT GOOD.
FSSSSSSSSSSSH!
HELP! HELP! HELP!

HELP! HELP! HELP!
REGINA?
REGINA! REGINA!
REGINA! REGINA!
PRIS! I'M IN HERE!
PRIS! PRIS!
REGINA! OH, THANK GOD YOU'RE OKAY!
I WAS SO WORRIED!

UH, PRIS?
HM?
COULD YOU GET ME DOWN?
OH. RIGHT.
HOW DID YOU FIND ME?
YOU'RE NOT GONNA BELIEVE THIS BUT I THINK FLAN LED ME HERE.
FLAN?

THE ONE AND ONLY. WHERE ARE WE ANYWAY?
AN OLD WEATHER STATION.
WHY?

NOW IT'S MY TURN TO SAY, "YOU'RE NOT GONNA BELIEVE THIS."
THE CREEPY GUY FROM BEFORE, HE BUILT A WEATHER MACHINE . . . CLOUD SEEDING OR SOMETHING . . . I'M NOT SURE.

BEFORE TONIGHT, I WOULD'VE SAID YOU WERE CRAZY, BUT NOW, SURE. WEATHER MACHINE. LET'S GO WITH THAT.
WAIT, WHERE IS HE?
LAST I SAW HIM, HE HEADED DOWN THERE.
OH . . . OH.
WELL, LET'S GET GOING!
WAIT! WE HAVE TO STOP THE MACHINE!
ARE YOU KIDDING? HAVEN'T WE BEEN THROUGH ENOUGH?
BESIDES, IT'S PROBABLY NOT EVEN REAL, REGINA! HE'S CRAZY!
PRIS, IT'S REAL. AND WE HAVE TO STOP IT. PLEASE. TRUST ME.
FINE. FINE. HOW DO WE TURN IT OFF?

OF COURSE.

IF YOU FEEL TWO TUGS ON THIS ROPE, PULL ME BACK, OKAY?
THREE TUGS. GOT IT.

FUNNY.
SORRY! SORRY! TWO TUGS!

WAIT! HERE! USE THIS TO FLIP THE BREAKER.
HUH? WHY?

SO YOU, UH, DON'T GET ELECTROCUTED.
YOU DO KNOW I'M GOING TO BE FULLY SUBMERGED IN WATER, RIGHT?
YEAH, BUT EVERY LITTLE BIT HELPS.

RIGHT. EVERY LITTLE BIT.

OH, AND UH, REGINA?
YEAH?
NOTHING. NEVER MIND.

LOVE YA, TOO, SIS.

SNAP

SNAP

KRAKA-THOOOOOOOOM

GNH-HUUUUUUUUH!
AAH!
REGINA! RUN!
PRIS! WHAT-WHAT-WHAT . . .

REGINA! I SAID, RU—
AAAAAHHH!
NO! STOP! WHAT ARE YOU DOING!
TAKING WHAT YOU DON'T DESERVE.

ARF!
ARF!
ARF!
HUH?
FLAN!

OOF!
FLAN! YOU'RE BACK! YOU SAVED US!
FLAN! YOU— HOLD ON! YOU'RE NOT FLAN!

UHHHH, IS IT SUPPOSED TO BE DOING THAT?
DANGER . . . OVERLOAD IMMINENT?
REGINA, WHAT DO YOU . . . REGINA?
WHAT ARE YOU DOING? RUN!
WHAT?

HOW'D YOU FIND US?
I'M HONESTLY NOT SURE MYSELF.
NOT TOO HARD TO SEE A FIREBALL THAT BIG.
WHAT HAPPENED IN THERE ANYWAY?
ARF!
WHO'S A GOOD BOY? WHO'S A GOOD BOY?
AREN'T YOU? AREN'T YOU A GOOD BOY?
PANT -PANT- PANT -PANT-
REGINA! PRIS!
GIRLS!

I'M SO GLAD YOU'RE ALL RIGHT!
WHAT HAPPENED? ARE YOU OKAY?
WE'RE FINE! WE'RE FINE!
PRIS WAS INCREDIBLE.
ARF! ARF! ARF!
AND WHO ARE YOU? OH. WOW. HE LOOKS JUST LIKE . . .
HEY, YOU GOTTA SEE THIS! SOME KIND OF CRAZY MACHINE IN HERE!
WHAT IS IT?
I HAVE NO IDEA!

HEY! LOOK! THE RAIN STOPPED!
YEAH.

IT SURE DID.

FRAN!
FRANNIE!

FRANGIPANE!
COME HERE!

REGINA!
REGINA!

WHAT?
FRAN WAS IN MY ROOM AGAIN!
AW! HE LIKES YOU!

CAN YOU JUST KEEP HIM OUT OF THERE, PLEASE?
HE CHEWS ON EVERY-THING.

AWW, DID SHE ALREADY FORGET THAT YOU SAVED HER LIFE? DID SHE?

NO, I JUST . . . JUST KEEP HIM OUT OF MY ROOM. PLEASE?
SIGH. YOU'RE A GOOD BOY, FRAN. THANKS AGAIN FOR SAVING MY LIFE.

WAIT! PRIS!

WHAT'S UP?

YOU DON'T THINK HE'S STILL OUT THERE, DO YOU?
WHO? MR. PETERSON? REGINA. HE'S DEAD.
THEN HOW COME THEY NEVER FOUND A BODY?
REGINA, RELAX. HE'S GONE. I PROMISE.
AND THE RAVEN MAN?

THERE WAS NO RAVEN MAN. IT WAS JUST MR. PETERSON IN A COSTUME.
AT LEAST, I'M PRETTY SURE.
BUT . . .

TELL YOU WHAT, WHY DON'T I SLEEP IN HERE TONIGHT?
YOU DON'T—
IT'S FINE. I WANT TO.

TAP TAP TAP TAP TAP

TAP TAP TAP TAP TAP TAP TAP

TAP TAP TAP TAP TAP TAP TAP TAP
SZNORT!
SZZZZZZNORT
SZZZZZNNNN

HNH? WHAT . . .
SCOOCH OVER.
MHM. G'NIGHT.

ZAC GORMAN is an author and cartoonist from Michigan. He received an Emmy for his work on Over the Garden Wall (Outstanding Animated Series, 2015) and was nominated for an Annie Award for his character design work on *Welcome to the Wayne*. His webcomic *Magical Game Time* was archived by the Library of Congress.

DAVE BARDIN is an award-winning illustrator who has worked in comics, commercials, music videos, video games, magazines, television, and book publishing. He has illustrated over twenty children's books, including titles for Bad Robot, Graphic India, Leap Frog, Little Brown, Scholastic, Pearson, ABDO, Cartoon Network, Marvel, and DC. He lives and works in Los Angeles.

IT'S A TYPICAL NIGHT IN THE TOWN OF RAVEN BROOKS . . .

ELEVEN-YEAR-OLD REGINA RELAXES AT HOME, HER FATHER AND STEPMOTHER ON A DATE WHILE HER OLDER STEPSISTER PRIS BABYSITS. BUT WHEN AN EMERGENCY ALERT COMES OVER THE AIRWAVES, THE TWO MUST GRAB THEIR THINGS AND HEAD OUT OF TOWN—A FLASH FLOOD IS COMING, CELL PHONE TOWERS ARE DOWN, AND THEY ARE ON THEIR OWN. AND TO MAKE THINGS WORSE, A FREAK CAR ACCIDENT LEAVES THEM STRANDED ON THE SIDE OF THE ROAD. CAN THE TWO YOUNG GIRLS MAKE IT TO SAFETY BEFORE THE FLOOD? AND JUST WHO IS THE STRANGE FIGURE THAT SEEMS TO BE TRAILING THEM EVERY STEP OF THE WAY?

IT'S AN ALL-NEW, FRIGHTENINGLY FUN STORY THAT TIES DIRECTLY INTO THE NEWEST *HELLO NEIGHBOR* GAME!

Cover Art by Dave Bardin
Cover Design by Jess Meltzer

MIDDLE GRADE
Ages 8 through 12

$12.99 US / $16.99 CAN / £7.99 UK

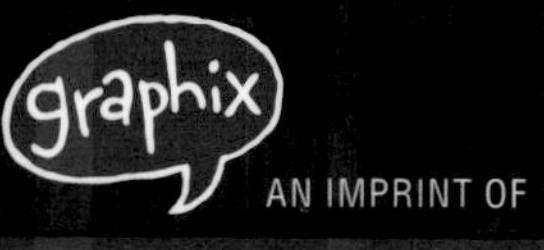

AN IMPRINT OF
SCHOLASTIC
scholastic.com

ISBN 978-1-338-72676-3
51299
9 781338 726763